MR. STINGY

by Roger Hargreaves

PRICE STERN SLOAN

An Imprint of Penguin Group (USA) Inc.

Mr. Stingy lived up to his name.

He lived in what could have been a nice house, but wasn't. He never painted it, or mended the windows, or repaired the roof.

Inside it was the same. No carpets! No curtains! No pictures! No fires!

And Mr. Stingy was so stingy, he made his furniture out of old orange boxes, and then complained about the price of nails!

Why, he was so stingy, do you know what he gave his brother for Christmas last year?

A piece of coal!

It wasn't as if Mr. Stingy didn't have any money.

Oh no!

He had lots of money, and he kept it all hidden in a box which he kept in the kitchen.

Every evening, he'd sit there counting it. It was the only thing Mr. Stingy liked doing.

But would he spend it?

Oh dear me, no.

Not old Stingy.

Not if he could help it!

One day, Mr. Stingy was sitting in his gloomy kitchen having a gloomy meal.

He only ever had one meal a day, and that day, he was having a cup of water and a piece of bread that was three weeks old.

Suddenly, he was interrupted by a knock at the door.

"Drat!" he said, because he didn't like people. "Drat and bother!"

He opened the door, and there, on his doorstep, stood a wizard.

A rather fat wizard.

"Hello," said the wizard. "I wonder if, by any chance, as it's such a warm day, you could possibly, if it's not too much trouble, be so kind as to, if it's not inconvenient, perhaps, as I'm very thirsty, provide me with, do you think, a glass, if it's not too much to ask, of water, please?"

He was a very wordy wizard.

"No!" replied Mr. Stingy rudely, and shut the door in his face.

And he went back into his kitchen to finish his meager meal.

But there, standing in front of him, was the wizard.

"How did you get in?" gasped Mr. Stingy.

"Well," replied the wizard, "it was by, how shall I put it, I just, well, you know, waved the old whatsitsname, magic wand don't you know, and, well, here I am, if you know what I mean!"

"You must be very poor," he remarked kindly, looking around.

"Oh, yes I am," lied Mr. Stingy.

"Then perhaps I can help you," said the wizard, pulling up a box to sit down on.

The box didn't move, so the wizard pulled it harder, and this time it did move. In fact, it tipped up and spilled all Mr. Stingy's money all over the floor.

"Well well well," exclaimed the wizard, eyeing the money rolling all over the kitchen floor. "Well well well well well well!"

"It would appear to me," he continued, "that you, sir, are an old stingypants!"

Mr. Stingy didn't hear him.

He was too busy scrabbling all over the floor trying to pick up his money.

"And stingypants," added the wizard, "need to be taught a lesson!"

So saying, he waved his magic wand.

All the money turned into potatoes!

Potatoes!

Poor Mr. Stingy.

"Oh! Oh dear! Oh dear me!" he wailed. "Please turn my money back into money. Oh please, please, please," he begged.

"Perhaps," replied the wizard. "But, on the other hand, taking all things into account, by and large, things being what they are, on the face of it, perhaps not."

"However," continued the wordy wizard, "if you make me a solemn promise never to be stingy again, then I will turn your money back into money. But," he added sternly, "if you are ever stingy again, then it's, how can I put it, then it's potatoes for you, my lad. If not other vegetables as well!"

Then the wizard had the glass of water he'd come for in the first place, except it was a cup of water because Mr. Stingy didn't have any glasses.

Then, with another wave of his wand, he turned the potatoes back into money, and another wave of his wand made himself disappear.

"Stupid wizard," muttered Mr. Stingy, picking up all his money.

The following day, Mr. Stingy decided to walk to town.

He never took the bus because that cost money!

On the way, he met an old washerwoman carrying an enormous bundle of washing.

"Please, kind sir," she asked, "could you possibly help me to carry this washing? It's so heavy!"

"No!" replied Mr. Stingy. "It's your washing. You carry it!"

But, as soon as he'd said that, he felt a tingling in his nose.

Mr. Stingy's nose turned into a carrot!!

"Oh no!" he gasped.

The old washerwoman chuckled.

And then Mr. Stingy remembered the wizard's words.

"Yes! Yes!" he cried in a panic. "Of course I'll help you!"

And he carried the huge bundle of washing to where the old washerwoman wanted.

And the carrot turned back into a nose, and off he went.

The old washerwoman chuckled again, and turned back into the wizard.

It had been him all along!

On his way into town, Mr. Stingy passed by a cottage garden.

In the garden there was an old man chopping wood. He saw Mr. Stingy going past and called out.

"Excuse me," he called. "Could you give an old man a bit of a hand, young fellow-me-lad?"

"No!" replied Mr. Stingy. "It's your wood. You chop it!"

But, as soon as the words had passed his lips, guess what happened?

His ears turned into tomatoes!!

"Oh no!" he gasped.

The old man chuckled.

And Mr. Stingy remembered the wizard's words.

"Yes! Yes!" he cried. "Of course I'll give you a hand."

And he chopped and chopped until all the wood was cut.

And the tomatoes turned back into ears, and off he went.

The old man chuckled again, and turned back into the wizard.

He was teaching Mr. Stingy a lesson, just as he'd promised.

Eventually Mr. Stingy arrived in the town.

There was a little boy crying because his ball had gotten stuck on top of a wall.

"Please, sir," cried the boy. "Please, sir, could you reach my ball down for me?"

"No!" retorted Mr. Stingy. "It's your ball. You . . ." Then he stopped.

There was a funny tingling feeling in his feet.

"Yes! Yes!" he said hurriedly. "Of course I will."

And he reached up and passed the ball to the boy, and went on his way, looking anxiously at his feet.

The little boy stopped crying and turned into the wizard.

"I think," he said to himself, "I think that Mr. Stingy, by and large, is beginning, if I'm not very much mistaken, to not be quite so stingy, and, I think, although I could be wrong, although I never am, that he has, thank goodness, learned his lesson."

Today he's nothing like so stingy as he used to be.

And he doesn't keep his money in a box in the kitchen anymore.

He spent it all on having his house mended and painted and made spick-and-span.

And he's turned into quite a generous sort of a fellow.

Goodness, he's so generous, do you know what he gave his brother last Christmas?

Two pieces of coal!